SEARCH FOR SCOOBY SNACKS

by Robin Wasserman

Illustrated by Duendes del Sur

Hello Reader - Level 1

ISBN 0-439-16166-5

40 39   40   11 12 13 14/0

Cover designed by Madalina Stefan and Mary Hall

Interiors designed by Mary Hall

Printed in the U.S.A.

First Scholastic printing, March 2000

SCHOLASTIC INC.

New York Toronto London Auckland Sydney
Mexico City New Delhi Hong Kong

and his friends were

camping at the .

The was bright.

There were no in the sky.

"Like, this is fun, but I'm

hungry!" said.

The 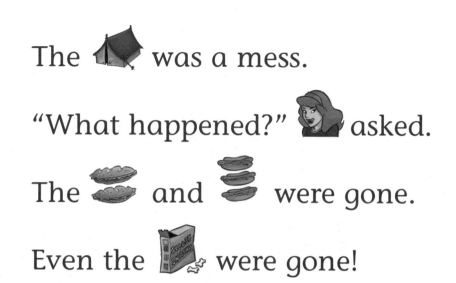 was a mess.

"What happened?" asked.

The and were gone.

Even the were gone!

"It looks like a  did this," said.

"A ?" asked.

"Oh, no!" said . He hid inside the .

"Ruh-roh!" said . He hid under a .

"We need to look for clues," said.

"It is the only way to find the missing ," said.

was scared. But he was also hungry.

"Let's go find that and get our food back!" said.

found a clue.

She found big .

 thought they looked like

monster .

 found a clue, too.

She found her on the

ground.

"Jinkies!" said. "I have a

hunch about who took our

food."

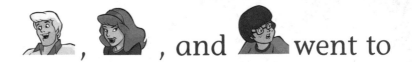, and went to

get Park Ranger Adams.

 and  sat on a  .

"I wish that I had a  ,"

 said.

 wished he had some .

"Like, all this waiting is making

me hungry," said.

"Let's go find some food!"

 shouted.

 used his to find the

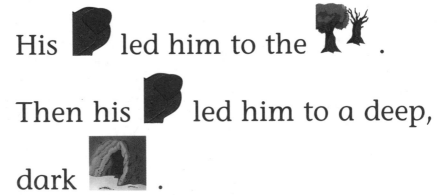 .

His led him to the .

Then his led him to a deep,

dark .

Scooby looked in the  .

Maybe there was a or a

in the cave.

"Maybe the are in the

," said.

went into the .

There was a big pile of food,

and the were on top!

Then  heard a noise.

Was it the ?

It was not a .

It was a big, brown .

"Run!" and shouted.

ran away.

But the grabbed 's tail.

The 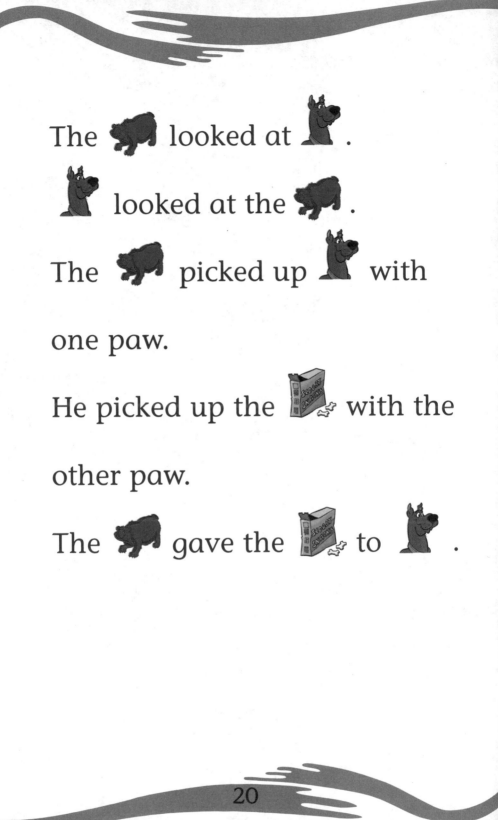 looked at ⬛ .

⬛ looked at the ⬛ .

The ⬛ picked up ⬛ with

one paw.

He picked up the ⬛ with the

other paw.

The ⬛ gave the ⬛ to ⬛ .

 brought the gang and

Ranger Adams back to help.

But did not need any help.

"Looks like we found our ,"

said.

"And found his ,"

said.

"Scooby-Dooby-Doo!"

barked.

Did you spot all the picture clues in this Scooby-Doo mystery?

Each picture clue is on a flash card. Ask a grown-up to cut out the flash cards. Then try reading the words on the back of the cards. The pictures will be your clue.

Reading is fun with Scooby-Doo!

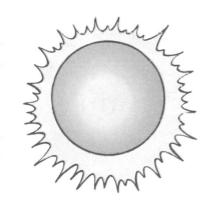

lake	Scooby
clouds	sun
Daphne	Shaggy

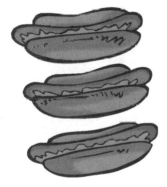

sandwiches	tent
Scooby Snacks	hot dogs
Velma	monster

bush	van
footprints	Fred
rock	book

nose	pizza
cave	trees
bear	bat